True Graffiti

by Danny Campbell
and Kimberly Campbell

Illustrated by William Presing

True Graffiti is hand-illustrated by the same Grade A Quality Jumbo artists who bring you *Disney's Doug*, the television series.

New York

Original characters for "The Funnies" developed by
Jim Jinkins and Joe Aaron.

Printed in the United States of America.

1 3 5 7 9 10 8 6 4 2

The artwork for this book was prepared using pen and ink.

The text for this book is set in 13-point Leewood.

Library of Congress Catalog Card Number: 99-67851

ISBN 0-7868-4383-7

CONTENTS

Doug Funnie was hurrying to get to school. He had left his favorite Man O' Steel Man comic book in his locker, and he wanted to finish it before class. As he rounded the corner of the main hallway of Beebe Bluff Middle School, he noticed a large crowd standing around.

I wonder what's going on, Doug thought, his detective instincts kicking in.

In the center of the crowd stood the girl of his dreams, Patti Mayonnaise. She didn't look at all like her normal, cheery self.

"Hey, Patti. What's . . ." Doug stopped

short. There on the wall, in bright orange letters, was **Patti Mayonnaise has the face of a Hyena.**

"Oh, Doug," gasped Patti. "Who would write such a mean thing?"

"Don't worry, Patti," Doug told her. "I'll find out the identity of the Phantom Scribbler."

Without even looking at Doug, Patti ran down the hall, trying to hide her face with her books.

"Wow, man, look at that!" a voice said from behind. It was Skeeter Valentine, Doug's best human friend. "Patti doesn't look anything like a hyena."

"That's for sure," Doug answered.

"What are you going to do, Doug?" Skeeter asked.

Patti Mayonnaise has the face of a Hyena

"I'm not going to rest until I find out who did this," Doug said. "He won't be defaming Patti Mayonnaise on the walls of Beebe Bluff Middle School on my watch!"

Doug touched the writing on the wall. "Hey, Skeet! Look at this stuff on my hands!"

"Looks like chalk," observed Skeeter.

"Orange chalk," Doug concluded. "I think we've found our first clue."

Later that day, Skeeter and Doug sat together during study hall. Doug pulled out the little notebook that he used to write down the clues of the various mysteries he investigated. He was now using it to list

his only clue and possible suspects, who at that point could be anybody.

"Gee, Doug, who would want to write on the walls of the school?" Skeeter asked. "Especially about Patti."

"I don't know," said Doug. "That's what makes this case so baffling."

Skeeter tried to puzzle it out. "It could be Roger, because . . . well . . . because he's Roger."

"No way, man," countered Doug. "Roger couldn't spell *hyena* if his life depended on it."

The final bell rang. Doug and Skeeter headed to their lockers. As they walked down the hallway, they almost collided with Fentruck as he rushed past them, a little late for a Bluffington Junior Yodelers

practice session. Fentruck didn't see them because he was trying to stuff the last of his cheesy curls into his mouth before he had to yodel.

"Doug, did you see Fentruck? He had some orange dust on his pants! You don't suppose he did it, do you?" Skeeter whispered.

"Nah," Doug replied. "Fentruck's always eating those orange cheesy curls, so he always has orange stuff on his pants where he wipes his hands. Besides, he's too nice."

"He really ought to lay off those cheesy curls," Skeeter honked.

Just as they reached the library, they

were greeted with another message in orange chalk. Scrawled over the doorway of the library, it read **Skeeter Valentine glides like a goat.**

"Oh, man!" said Skeeter. "Now it's my name up in chalk!"

"Another crime," said Doug, staring at the message. "And another clue. Now we know that the Scribbler knows both you and Patti."

Leaving the building, Doug and Skeeter saw Patti running toward them and waving. "Doug! Skeeter! Did you see what someone wrote on the wall at the library?"

"Yeah," Doug answered. "We've got to find out who did this before he strikes again."

"Who knows who could be next?"

lamented Skeeter. And with that, the three of them headed home.

The next day at school Skeeter and Doug passed the art room. Doug stopped short. Inside the room was a big box of orange chalk.

"Did you see what I saw, Skeet?" asked Doug. "A major clue!"

"Let's go in and see what else we can find out," Skeeter responded.

They slipped into the art room and froze in strange, twisted poses, pretending to be modern art sculptures while they surreptitiously looked around. Finally certain that they were alone, they pounced on the box of chalk. There was a note on it that read DO NOT TOUCH: RESERVED FOR ADVANCED ART CLASS/THURSDAY.

"Hello, Doog!" a voice shouted. It was Fentruck, surrounded by a cloud of orange dust.

"What are you doing in here?" asked Doug.

"I am delivering special chalk for our advanced art class. It comes from my native country, Yakestonia, the birthplace of fine chalk. Good-bye, Doog and Skeeter, my friends."

"Bye." Doug waved as they followed Fentruck out of the room.

"I didn't know chalk was born in Yakestonia," Skeeter said.

"I didn't know chalk was born at all," said Doug. "Wait a minute! This could be a clue! Whoever the Scribbler is, he must be in Thursday's advanced art class!"

Most of the people in that class were eighth graders. The only seventh graders in the class besides Doug were Skunky and Fentruck. Sally from the newspaper staff was also in that class.

"Well, it's not Skunky," said Doug. "He couldn't concentrate long enough to do it."

"Maybe it's Sally," Skeeter said.

"Sally?" repeated Doug. "It can't be Sally!"

"Why don't we go over to the newspaper room and check it out right now?" Skeeter said.

As Doug and Skeeter entered the newspaper room, Sally was working at a computer while Patti and Guy looked over a layout. "Patti, can we talk to you?" asked Doug.

"Sure," Patti said. "What's going on?"

They walked out into the hallway, narrowly missing a collision with

Fentruck, who was trying to yodel through the cheesy curls stuffed in his mouth.

Doug looked at Skeet, then took a deep breath. "Patti," he asked, "how well do you know Sally?"

Patti looked surprised. "Doug Funnie, you think she's the Scribbler? You have the wildest imagination! Sally's one of my friends—and she's allergic to chalk. She told me about the sneezing attack she had in art class the day Skunky banged the erasers together."

"Oh, yeah, I remember that," said Doug. He gave Skeet a look and scratched Sally's name off his suspect list.

"Doug?" asked Patti. "Can

I help you and Skeeter find the Phantom Scribbler?"

Immediately, Doug was thrown into a fantasy. He and Patti, roaming the halls of Beebe Bluff Middle School together, searching every nook and cranny with a magnifying glass built for two. "Oh, Doug, you're so . . . Sherlock Holmes-y," she would sigh, prompting Doug to respond,

"Elementary, my dear Patti."

"Doug?" repeated Patti. "Are you all right? Are you listening to me?"

Back in reality, Doug replied, "Sure. We need all the help we can get."

Just then, the bell rang. As they made their way down the hall, they ran into Beebe Bluff. "Doug! You'd better get over to the gymnasium right away!"

Doug, Skeeter, and Patti ran to the gym and saw, once again, a message scrawled across the wall in orange chalk: **Doug Funnie smells like a warthog's snout.**

"Skeeter, who would write such a mean thing about me?" Doug cried. "What does a warthog's snout smell like, anyway?"

"I don't know man, but it can't smell good," Skeeter said.

At that moment, the janitor walked in, bucket and sponge in hand. "You kids better get to class! I've got enough trouble cleaning up after that kid with the chalk."

"You know who did this?" they asked, almost simultaneously.

"I just saw him running down the hall covered in orange dust from the chalk."

"Aha!" shouted Doug, realizing who the perpetrator was.

"Eureka!" shouted Skeeter.

"You know who it is, too?" asked Doug.

"No," Skeeter replied. "I just like the sound of that word. Eureka! Eureka! Hey! How could we have missed someone covered in orange chalk dust?"

Pulling out his notebook, Doug said, "The Scribbler is someone who can be covered in orange dust without attracting attention. He's in Thursday's advanced art class. He knows you, me, and Patti. And his chosen medium is . . . fine Yakestonian chalk."

Will Doug ever erase the mystery of the Phantom Scribbler from the halls of Beebe Bluff Middle School?

Doug, Skeeter, and Patti left the gymnasium and ran back down the main hallway, following a trail of orange dust. They found only Fentruck in the music room. He was delighted to see them.

"Surprise, Doog, Patti, and Skeeter! Happy Yip Yip Day!"

"Happy what?" the three friends asked.

"Yip Yip Day. In my country every year on Yip Yip Day, we write special things about our friends on the walls of public buildings. Later, we celebrate with cakes and punchy. Is it not grand, Doog?"

"So that's why you wrote those things on the walls," Patti said. "I never knew you thought I looked like a hyena."

"Oh, yes. The hyena is the happiest animal in our country, and you are always

smiling, Patti." Fentruck turned to Skeeter. "And you roll so smoothly into trees on your rolling board that I thought of the

most surefooted animal in my country, the goat."

"Fentruck," Doug said. "Why did you say I smell like a warthog's snout?"

"In my country, warthog snouts are more valuable than gold. The Yakestonians actually trade them like money. My own father's house he purchased for three snouts! When we speak of smelling like the warthog's snout, it is the highest compliment. You, Doog, are more valuable than a herd of warthog snouts."

"Thank you, Fentruck. That's the nicest thing anybody has ever said about me . . . I think," said Doug. "And happy Yip Yip Day!"

THE CASE OF THE MOOCHING MARTIANS

Doug Funnie had been working all day and most of the previous night. As First Assistant Beet Fryer of the Bill Bluff Biennial Beet Fry, he was, to put it mildly, "beet." His family all went out for dinner, but Doug wanted to stay home.

After downing a hot dog and chips, Doug decided to watch the Tri-County Swimming Championships. When he turned on the television, it was showing a commercial with an unusual jingle for Martin's Aerodynamic Racing Suits. He'd already missed the last race. Doug turned

MARTIN'S
BEET FRY

off the television but kept on humming the strange tune he'd just heard—he couldn't get it out of his head.

The next day, as he was walking home from school, Doug saw the Sleeches pushing a wheelbarrow piled high with cans of Mexicali beet salsa and more beet juice than Doug had ever seen. It also held an old microwave, aluminum foil, a "Beet-boy" computer game, and three TVs, all with broken antennae. The Sleeches were humming the same tune that Doug had been

unable to get out of his head since the night before. For a moment Doug wondered if the music were coming from the wheelbarrow.

Doug called out to them, "Al, Moo, what are you doing?"

Al and Moo froze. They looked at each other. "Sixty-eight!" whispered Al.

"Seventy-two!" Moo agreed. They grabbed the wheelbarrow and ran like the wind. When a toaster fell off onto the sidewalk, they didn't even stop to pick it up.

"What's going on with them?" Doug wondered aloud.

"Beats me," said a voice behind him. It was Skeeter. "They came to my house last night asking if I had a blender they could borrow. I gave them an old toaster. They seemed happy with it. But this seems

weird, even for the Sleeches! What do you think they're doing?"

"We won't know unless we follow the wheelbarrow!" said Doug.

So Doug and Skeeter trailed Al and Moo through town, all the way out to the Lucky Duck Lake RV Park.

As they got close to the lake, Doug heard a familiar tune playing softly in the distance. He immediately started humming along. He didn't even realize he was doing it until Skeeter started honking along, too—off-key.

Suddenly, Doug pointed toward the park. "Skeet, look at that! That's not a trailer, is it?"

"If it is, it's the strangest one I've ever seen," Skeeter said.

They moved closer. The vehicle had a huge fin on top and was covered with antennae. It was cigar-shaped and shining—just like a UFO!

"Hey, man! What's that?" asked Doug. "A flying saucer in Lucky Duck RV Park?"

"I guess they heard about the beet fry," answered Skeeter.

Just then, Al and Moo knocked on the UFO's door and two beings emerged from

the craft. Short and bald, they were dressed funny and obviously not from Earth. Just like the vehicle they came from, their clothing had a fin on the back. They seemed to have two sets of eyes. The second set was black and popped up out of their foreheads.

"Doug?" asked Skeeter. "They look like . . . aliens."

"I know," said Doug.

"What are they doing with Al and Moo?"

"Visiting family?" Doug suggested.

"That would explain a lot," said Skeeter.

Doug and Skeeter crept closer. The aliens were waving their arms at Al and Moo. They appeared to be agitated.

Doug and Skeeter noticed what looked

like a monogram on their spacesuits. It matched the letters on their "spacecraft." From what Doug could see, there were four letters: M—A—R—S. "MARS?!?" Doug gasped. "Let's get out of here!"

Skeeter was already gone.

Doug finally caught up with him close to the Funnies' house. "What do you think about all this, Skeet?" Doug asked.

"I think I'm staying away from Lucky Duck RV Park," answered Skeeter. "And from Al and Moo. I don't want to be vaporized."

"Neither do I," said Doug, opening the door to his house. "Boy, that was some strange-looking vehicle, wasn't it?"

Doug turned on the television. The commercial for Martin's Aerodynamic Racing Suits was playing again. He turned the TV right off, but he still thought he could hear the strange music.

"Al and Moo sure seemed happy to see those aliens," Skeeter said.

"Yeah," Doug agreed. "Maybe this is the mother ship they've been expecting. But why would aliens from outer space want to stay in an RV Park? And what's that music I keep hearing in my head?!?"

"You're hearing music, too? Oh, man!

That's a relief!" Skeeter sighed. "I thought I was the only one being taken over by aliens."

Doug frowned. "We've both been hearing strange music, like the kind in the commercial for Martin's Aerodynamic Racing Suits. Al and Moo are collecting food and appliances to bring to a strange craft in the RV park. The craft has MARS written on the side, just like on their fin suits. And they have an extra set of superlaser eyes. Probably to vaporize enemies—that's us."

Then Doug said something very strange. "Skeeter, I want to go back to the RV park. Are you with me?"

Skeeter honked his consent. "But," he said, "if aliens take over my brain, I'm really gonna be bummed out."

Doug and Skeeter crept into the RV park. Sure enough, at the door of the craft stood Al and Moo Sleech, each with a wheelbarrow full of beet-flavored pop 'n' toast tarts and fax machines.

Like before, the beings were waving their arms and shaking their heads at the Sleeches. If Doug didn't know better, he would have thought they were telling them to go away.

Suddenly, Skeeter sneezed loudly. Al, Moo, and the creatures turned around.

Doug and Skeeter were busted.

Are Doug and Skeeter about to be vaporized? Have Al and Moo been taken over by four-eyed, finned Martians?

"Let's get out of here, Skeet," Doug whispered. They turned to run away, but Skeeter tripped over a vine, stumbled, and knocked them both down right in front of the Martians.

"Please! Don't melt my brain with your laser eyes!" begged Skeeter.

"Friends of yours?" an alien asked Al and Moo with a sigh.

The Sleeches said nothing.

"Yes, yes, we're friends of theirs. Don't zap us!" Doug said. "I am Doug Funnie, and this is my friend Skeeter Valentine. We come in peace."

"Not again!" cried the smaller of the beings, perhaps a female. "Kids, please! We aren't aliens!"

"You're not?" Doug and Skeeter gasped.

"No!" stated the larger being. "My name is Joe Frem. This is my wife, Fran. We work for Martin's Aerodynamic Racing Suits—'MARS' for short. We're here for the Tri-County Swimming Championships. Our heads are shaved to test the water drag of these new suits. This is our latest model, with supergoggles. Surely, you've heard the MARS song." He opened the door to the trailer, and a familiar jingle started playing.

"That's the music I keep hearing!" Doug shouted.

"Yeah. It's part of our new swimwear launch," responded Mr. Frem. "Catchy, isn't it?"

"Not possible!" said Al. "Our calculations indicate a UFO landed in this spot three days ago. That is just when you arrived. You are from the planet Mars. Our charts confirm it."

Moo added, "We are never wrong."

"You guys," Doug laughed. "Maybe you should recalculate."

"Not necessary," Al insisted. "We will

go home now. We know your mission is too important to reveal to our friends."

"Tomorrow we will bring more samples of Earth cuisine and technology," Moo said. The Sleeches took their wheelbarrows and left.

Mr. Frem heaved a sigh and turned to Doug. "Please tell me they're not going to bring back more wheelbarrows full of junk."

"I think that's exactly what they're going to do," Doug replied.

Mr. Frem shook his head. "Honey," he said. "Let's skip the beet fry and get out of town tonight!"

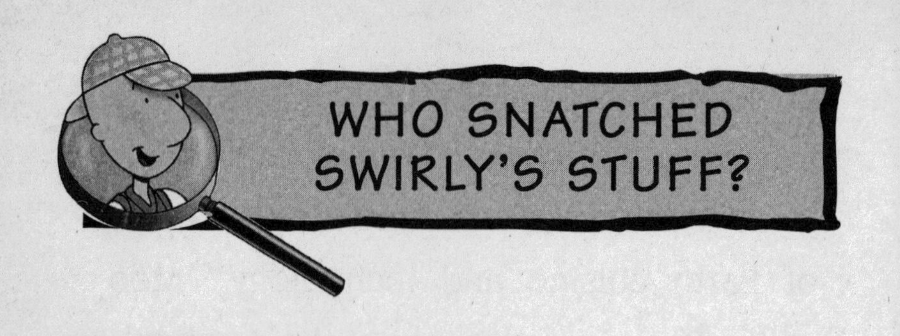

WHO SNATCHED SWIRLY'S STUFF?

It had been a long day at Beebe Bluff Middle School. After taking three pop quizzes and finishing his English composition, "I Remember Bloatsburg," Doug wanted to have some fun. He asked Skeeter to go to Lucky Duck Park and play beetball for a while, but Skeeter said he had something he had to do. So Doug decided to stop by Swirly's and treat himself to a Hot Fudge Nutty Banana Beet Swirly-Doo.

As he approached Swirly's, he saw

something that shocked him. Just as Mr. Swirly turned and went to the back of his shop, someone wearing a ski mask ran into the store, took three tubs of Swirly's "Choc-a-Boom" ice cream, and stumbled out the door. The thief tripped over his feet and fell to the ground, tearing his pants. Doug tried to follow him, but he was too fast. He grabbed the stolen ice cream and disappeared.

"Boy, I wish Skeeter were here. He could have caught this hoodlum on his skateboard," said Doug.

Doug ran back to Swirly's. "Mr. Swirly! Mr. Swirly! There's a Choc-a-Boom bandit in Bluffington!"

"Oh, hello, Douglas. What can I get for you today? Your favorite Hot Fudge

CHOC
BOOM

Nutty Banana Beet Swirly-Doo?" Mr. Swirly said, smiling.

"Mr. Swirly," Doug said, "I hate to be the one to tell you, but three tubs of your Choc-a-Boom ice cream have been stolen. But don't worry. I plan to go undercover to bring them back."

Mr. Swirly didn't even glance at the freezer. "Don't be silly, Doug," he said. "All my ice cream is present and accounted for."

Doug stared at the three empty spaces where the tubs used to be. He shook his head. Poor Mr. Swirly, he thought, he's in denial.

The case was so serious Doug left without his Swirly-Doo. "I'm glad I took those tae kwon dog courses with

Porkchop. I'll have to call upon all my detective skills to catch this ice cream criminal!" Doug said to himself as he came to the entrance to Lucky Duck Park. "The thief must be hiding somewhere in the park. Clearly this investigation calls for a master of disguises. Someone who can become anyone, anything, at any time. I think this is a job for . . . The Chameleon!" The Chameleon was one of Doug's favorite crime-fighting characters. He was able to solve cases by blending into the background.

"I have it! I'll disguise myself with leaves and make like a tree," Doug exclaimed. He covered himself with small leaves. Then he found twigs on the ground and stuck them into his sleeves

and pockets so they would stick out like tree branches. Confident in his treelike demeanor, Doug marched deeper into the park.

He had just positioned himself between two other trees when he noticed someone holding a ski mask, just like the thief's. "No! Not Patti Mayonnaise!" he whispered when he realized who it was. Could Doug really uphold his crimefighter's oath if it meant throwing the most perfect girl in the universe in the slammer? As Patti came closer, Doug assumed a convincing tree position.

"Hey, Doug," said Patti. "What are you doing with those leaves on you?"

Doug's branches drooped. Only Patti would be able to see through his clever

disguise. "Oh . . . hey, Patti," Doug said. "Nice day, isn't it? Why are you carrying a ski mask around?"

"I just found it a little while ago," Patti replied. "Do you know where the Lost and Found is? Somebody might be skiing without it."

Doug glanced downward and noted that Patti's pants weren't torn. With a sigh of relief, he decided that Patti was off his list of suspects. "Can I see the ski mask?" Doug asked. Patti handed it over and Doug examined it for clues. There was an ice cream stain above the mouth hole. "Just as I suspected!" he said. "Patti, let me take this. I know where it belongs."

"Sure, Doug. Thanks."

"By the way, Patti, was there anyone around when you found this?"

"Um . . . Skunky, Chalky, and Roger were over there by that tree," she said, pointing.

"Thanks, Patti," Doug called to her as he walked away.

"Roger!" Doug said to himself. "Roger

doesn't even like Choc-a-Boom. Why didn't he go for the Minty Green Slimeball, like always?"

"Hey, Funnie," said Roger. "What's with the landscaping?"

Doug quickly shed his leaves and branches. Just as he was about to question Roger, he noticed a tear in *Chalky's* pants! And then he saw an ice cream stain on the back of Chalky's shirt! Doug focused his attention on Chalky.

"What happened to your pants, Chalky?" he asked.

"Somebody zoomed

through here on a skateboard or something," Chalky sniffed. "I never knew what hit me."

"What about your shirt?" Doug said, pointing to the suspicious stain.

"Oh, no!" Chalky said. "This is my lucky shirt. That skateboard guy got some ice cream on me."

"You didn't see who it was, then," Doug said.

"It happened too fast. I heard him honk his horn, so he must have been trying to warn me."

Doug wrote down, "Honked his horn." Then he said, "Okay. Thanks, Chalky. See you later."

Doug headed home. As he walked, the events at Swirly's swirled through his

head. Someone has stolen some ice cream from Mr. Swirly, but he doesn't want to believe it. Patti found a ski mask on a warm, sunny day in the park, nowhere near a ski lodge. And whoever ran into Chalky on a skateboard honked first.

Doug reached his front door. On it, there was a note. The note read DOUG, I KNOW YOU'RE LOOKING FOR ME. MEET ME AT MR. SWIRLY'S AFTER 4:30.

Suddenly Doug knew the identity of the ice cream thief.

Will Mr. Swirly accept the loss of his ice cream? Will Doug catch the Choc-a-Boom thief before the evidence melts?

Doug ran as fast as he could to Swirly's. He had to get there by 4:30 to stop the thief before he struck again. As he ran, he asked himself what The Chameleon would do. He decided he would hide in one of the trash cans in the kitchen. When the thief came again, he would leap out and tae kwon dog him to the ground.

The first part of Doug's plan worked beautifully. He sneaked into the kitchen and hid in a recycling bin that fortunately had just been emptied and cleaned. The Chameleon was ready. Only seconds later, he heard running steps and the creak of the freezer opening.

"Halt!" he shouted, jumping out of the bin. "These feet are deadly weapons!" Unfortunately, Doug's sneaker caught the

top of the recycling bin, sending Doug and the bin rolling out the kitchen door and into the shop. As he struggled to his feet, he heard a crash.

Doug grabbed the thief by the ankles, wrestled him to the ground, and ripped off his mask to reveal . . . Skeeter Valentine!

"Skeeter, don't do it! Put them back before it's too late!" Doug shouted, collapsing on the floor. "Don't you see you're heading for a life of crime? This Choc-a-Boom addiction is a sickness. Fight it now!"

"Cut! What's that kid doing in here?" a voice boomed from above.

Doug opened his eyes and looked around. What were all those cameras doing in Swirly's?

"Hey, isn't that Judy Funnie's little brother?" The voice sounded sort of familiar.

"I don't care who he is, he just ruined our last scene and almost broke a camera. Now we'll have to shoot it again," another voice answered angrily.

"No," said a third voice. "Let's keep it. His dramatic attempt to turn his friend

away from a life of crime is truly heart-wrenching. We'll put him in the movie, too." Doug looked up and recognized three film students from the Moody School for the Gifted.

"Doug," Skeeter said, "I would have told you about the movie, but the director said not to talk to anybody about it until we finished my scene. It's about—"

One of the film students stepped

forward. "It's a semi-documentary about what can happen when the need for ice cream is thwarted," she said, "called *I Scream for Ice Cream*." She seemed to be sizing Doug up. "We can use you in another scene, too—about youths meeting their ice cream needs in a healthy way, with spoons. But"—she hesitated—"we'll do several takes. You'll have to eat a lot of ice cream—and make the audience believe you're enjoying it."

Doug smiled, picturing himself with an Oscar. He had never felt so confident. This was a role he could really sink his teeth into. "I think I can manage that," he said. "When do I start?"

The detective business would have to wait. He was headed for stardom!

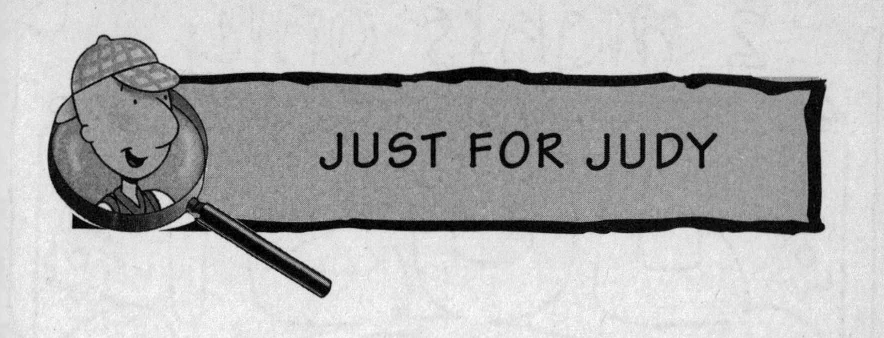

Doug and Porkchop sat on the front porch. The house had gotten a lot smaller since Judy did her one-woman show, *Just Judy.* Everyone in Bluffington was talking about it—according to Judy. Now she was trying to figure out what to do for an encore. "I just want to give my public what they want," she said. "More me."

Doug and Porkchop walked around the block for a while and then over to Swirly's for a chocolate shake and a Peanutty Buddy. While they were there, they saw Al and Moo.

2 nights only
JUST
JUDY
...

"Hello, Doug Funnie," the brothers chimed.

"Hey, guys," Doug answered.

"We would be glad to assist you again tomorrow," said Al.

Doug remembered. "Oh, yeah, my science project. 'The Effects of Happy Banjo Music on Beet Growth.' Thanks for offering to help me, guys. You've been more helpful than . . . well, than you needed to be."

"We will appear at 10:00 A.M. sharp, Doug Funnie. By the way, how is your sister, Judy Funnie?" asked Moo.

"Very annoying, thank you," answered Doug.

"We enjoyed her show," said Moo. "We laughed. We cried. We got dizzy."

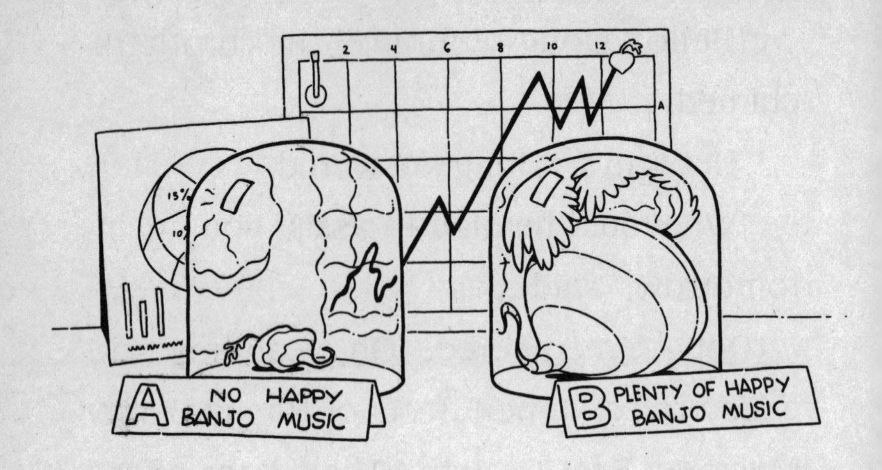

"Yes," said Al. "She is perfection in pants."

"Good-bye, Doug Funnie," they called.

When they figured Judy might be finished trying out various dramatic readings and interpretive dances, Doug and Porkchop headed back home. As they entered the house, they heard a screech.

"All right, Dougie, hand them over!" It was Judy and she meant business.

"Hand what over?" Doug asked, completely startled.

"You know what. My head shots—the picture of me I send out for auditions."

"Head shots? I don't know what you're talking about," Doug said.

"Don't play 'Who, me?' with me, you little thief! I knew you were jealous of my fame, but I didn't think you'd stoop so low as to steal." Judy turned to Porkchop sitting beside Doug. "And you!" she said.

Porkchop made a "who me?" gesture. She went on. "I expected no better from Doug, but I thought you had more class. *Et tu*, Porkchop? *Et tu?*" Judy ran off, slamming her bedroom door behind her.

Safe in his own room, Doug turned to Porkchop. "I'm beginning to suspect that someone has stolen Judy's head shots, Porkchop. And Judy's blaming us! We'll have to solve the case to clear our names—before Judy gets any weirder."

The next day at breakfast, Judy wasn't speaking to Doug, which Doug didn't mind at all, except when she wouldn't pass the sugar. After breakfast, Doug tried to question her, but Judy just pointed her finger at him and said, "*J'accuse*, Doug!" Then she ran to her room. She stayed up

there all morning, but she emerged for a brief moment to receive a standing ovation from the Sleech Brothers when they arrived.

Soon after the brothers left, Judy came running into Doug's room. "This time you've gone too far," she said.

"Now what?" Doug sighed. Porkchop put on his best innocent look.

"Whatever it is, Judy, I didn't do it. As a matter of fact, I've been trying to help you. Now, when was the last time you saw your . . ."

"My favorite feather boa! The one I wore in my show. You're trying to ruin my acting career, aren't you?"

"Listen, Judy, for the last time, I don't have your stuff, I don't *want* your stuff."

Judy's face suddenly softened. "I understand Doug. You can't help not only being a second child, but having such an extraordinary born-for-greatness older sibling."

As Judy returned to her room, Porkchop patted Doug's shoulder sympathetically with his paw.

"I still don't know who's taking Judy's

stuff—and why," Doug sighed. Porkchop shrugged and shook his head.

The next day Judy refused to speak a word to Doug or even say his name without sneering. Doug cheered up after he played some happy banjo music for his science project beet. Then, late in the afternoon, Al and Moo came by to work with him.

"Dougie, tell me the truth, do you have a death wish?" Judy asked, walking into the kitchen where the boys were working.

Al and Moo looked at each other. Moo spoke first. "Uh-oh. Twenty-nine."

"No, no," Al reacted. "Fifty-six!"

"Right," said Moo.

They spoke in perfect unison. "Doug Funnie, we must go."

"We are allergic to confrontation," Al finished. "Good-bye, Doug Funnie."

"Doug!" Judy bellowed.

Doug moaned. "What is it this time?"

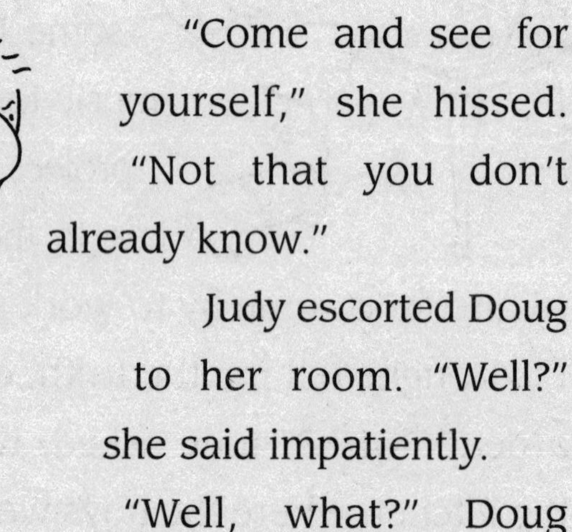

"Come and see for yourself," she hissed. "Not that you don't already know."

Judy escorted Doug to her room. "Well?" she said impatiently.

"Well, what?" Doug was getting impatient, too, by now. "You scared

off my friends to make me look at your room?"

"No. My veils are gone. The three veils I used in my interpretive dance about the phases of the moon. They've disappeared. Disappeared into thin air."

"Well, I can't help that," Doug said. "I'm sure your stuff didn't disappear by itself, but it's not my fault."

"Of course not," answered Judy sarcastically. "Oh, by the way, you were in the house each time my things were stolen."

Doug decided to ignore Judy's accusation. "Was anyone else here?"

Judy didn't even bother to think. "The only people who were here every time something got stolen were you and me, Mr. Who-Else-Can-I-Blame!"

"Judy! Come on, think! I didn't do it! And neither did you." He paused for a second. "And neither did Porkchop."

Porkchop tried to show Judy how innocent he was.

"There must have been someone else," Doug went on. "Think, Judy, think!"

After a moment, she said, "You know, I believe your little friends may have been here, too. What are their names? Fifty-two and Twenty-seven?"

Doug corrected her. "That's Al and Moo."

"Whatever," Judy said.

Doug wrote all the suspects' names in his notebook. "Thanks, Judy. Porkchop,

let's get going. We have a mystery to solve."

Doug went to his room and took out the notebook. "Okay, Porkchop, this is what we've got so far. It's only Judy's stuff that's missing. Everything that disappears goes missing in the afternoon, after school, while I'm busy working on my science project. Everything that was taken was connected to Judy's show. The same people were in the house every time. . . . Porkchop, I think I know who did it. But I can't understand why."

Will Doug be able to clear his name before Judy rubs him out? And what has happened to Judy's stuff?

On Saturday, Al and Moo came over to help Doug with his science project again. Shortly after arriving, they excused themselves to get some beet juice. Doug waited—then he followed them down the hall. He caught them standing in Judy's room.

"Hey, what are you guys doing?" demanded Doug.

"Oh, Doug Funnie, this is not what it looks like," said Al. He handed Doug a note he held in his hand. The note read:

Judy Funnie
we request your presence
at the first meeting of
The Judy Funnie Fan Club
tonight at 7:00 P.M.
at Swirly's.
We wish to pay tribute
to Bluffington's brightest teenage star
(you).

"We are sorry, Doug Funnie," said Al. "We hoped to surprise your sister at tonight's festivities with a full-scale diorama of *Just Judy* in midact. We needed the boa and the veils."

Doug asked, "What about the head shots?"

Al and Moo looked at each other guiltily. "The head shots were just for us," Moo confessed.

Judy, who had been listening from the hallway, burst into the room. "It's quite all right," she said. "Of course you needed those trifling little heirlooms to do justice to a display of my magnificence! Such awesome talent must have left you dumb-struck!" And with a sweeping bow, she concluded, "It will be my pleasure to

attend the opening of your gala little fan club."

"Oh, brother!" Doug rolled his eyes as Porkchop flopped to the floor.

DOUG'S EVIL TWIN

It had been a great day in Bluffington, and it was about to get better. Doug was going to Patti's beetball game this afternoon. Maybe he'd invite her to Swirly's for a strawberry Frothy Goat after they won.

As he neared the beetball field, Doug was busy trying to come up with a clever remark to say to Patti. Then he saw the team standing around her. They all turned and looked at him. None of them were smiling. Especially not Patti.

"Hey, Patti, ready to cream the Goatherders?" Doug called. Patti didn't even look at him. She didn't say anything. "Patti, what's wrong?" he asked.

"I saw you, Doug Funnie. You were climbing that tree," Patti said. "I headed over to say 'hey,' and the next thing I know, I'm being pelted with boosenberries. Now I'm a mess, and the coach won't let me play because the name and number on my uniform are covered by boosenberry juice! How could you, Doug?"

Beebe shook her fist at Doug. "We better not lose this game, or else! If we start losing, the coach will put me in and I'll get sweaty!" she bellowed.

All the other kids looked at him accusingly and muttered about how they'd

probably lose this game because of him.

Doug was completely confused. The entire beetball team was mad at him, and he hadn't even done anything. Worst of all, the love of his life was upset with him! "Patti," he protested, "you know I would never do something to make you lose the game."

"I don't want to believe that you would," said Patti. "But I saw you with my own eyes." Patti and her entire team turned their backs on Doug.

"How could she think it was *me* up in that tree?" Doug asked himself. "And how can I prove that it *wasn't* me?"

Just then, Doug saw Roger coming toward him. "Hey, Roger! Did you see anything unusual at the beetball field today?"

he asked, taking out his detective's notebook.

"Only you climbing a tree and heaving boosenberries at Patti Mayonnaise," Roger answered, as he strolled on.

"Perfect," Doug said. "Another witness against me."

Doug looked up to see Connie. She was covered in mud, and she was glaring at him. "Oh, hey, Connie," he said, trying to sound as nice as possible. "Where are you off to?"

"Nowhere, thanks to you!" she said. "Now that you've knocked me into a mud puddle and didn't even say you were sorry! Thanks a lot." She stalked off.

Doug sat down heavily on a nearby bench. He hoped no one else would come by. He had to try to make some sense of this mystery.

"What's going on?" he asked himself. "It's almost like I've got an evil twin out there trying to make me look bad—like that time Quailman was being tormented by . . . the Dark Quail."

Doug imagined himself in the giant made-up city of Megalopolis where Quailman and Quaildog fought evil, and good always triumphed. That is, until the Dark Quail showed up. "It's time to make a change for the worse!" hyuked the Dark Quail.

Zooming across the sky, throwing boosenberries on unsuspecting beetball players, blowing innocent bystanders into mud puddles, the Dark Quail flew, shouting, "It's time to unleash the powers of the Quail!" Under his breath, he muttered, "The Dark Quail, that is!"

The townspeople were frightened and panic-stricken. "Oh, no! Has Quailman gone mad? Who will save us from this evil, fowl-feathered tormentor?"

"And expensive dry cleaning bills?" another citizen added.

Back at the Thicket of Solitude, Quailman heard the cries of Megalopolis and soared to the scene. "Stop, you fiend!" Quailman shouted, circling the villain. "No one can bring evil into this town

while I'm here. Not even me."

"Oh, yeah? And what are you going to do about it, *Snailman*?" taunted the Dark Quail.

"That's Quailman with a 'Q U' to you, mister," Our Hero corrected. "I will stop you with pure good." As the Fine-Feathered Defender spoke, he slowly crept toward the Dark Quail, pouncing on him the instant he was in range.

"Hey, what are you doing?" asked the Dark Quail. I feel all warm and cuddly inside. I can't be the Dark Quail if I feel good! Stop it! I'm losing my edge!"

"This is called a hug," explained Quailman. "All the really nice people do it. Even manly superheroes can do it."

"Please stop it!" the Dark Quail begged. "I'm starting to feel . . . to feel . . . good! Oh, no! I'm melding . . . melding . . . melding . . ." and the Dark Quail was reabsorbed into Quailman.

THUD! "Ouch!" Doug, acting out his fantasy, had climbed up on top of the bench and slipped off, falling to the ground.

"Quailman wouldn't take the blame for something he didn't do!" Doug shouted, getting up.

He set out to restore his good name.

Doug hurried down the streets of Bluffington toward Skeeter's house. He

could see Skeeter up ahead, sitting on the side-walk and rubbing his head. Skeeter must have wiped out on his skateboard, again, thought Doug as he went to his friend.

"Hey, Skeet," greeted Doug. "Did you wipe out?"

"You know what happened," Skeeter accused him.

"Oh, no, not again!" said Doug. "Look, whatever you think I did, I didn't."

"You didn't sabotage my skateboard?" Skeeter said.

"Why would I do that?" Doug asked.

"I don't know, man," Skeeter said. "But

someone who looked a lot like you was messing with my skateboard. After I fell, I found a wad of bubble gum stuck up between the wheels."

"Skeeter, you've got to believe me! I didn't even have time to put gum on your skateboard. I was too busy not throwing boosenberries all over Patti and not pushing Connie into a mud puddle."

"Man, you've sure been busy not doing a lot of bad stuff," Skeeter gasped.

Doug extended his right hand to shake Skeeter's. "Trust me, Skeet . . ."

Skeeter shook his hand. "Cool, man," he said. "You had me worried there."

Doug pulled his detective's notebook out of his pocket. "Whoever pulled these stunts was at the beetball field with

Patti, and then on the street with Connie, and then in front of your house with you. Where exactly did you see the person who looked like me?" Doug interrogated.

"Right here." Skeeter pointed to a muddy footprint. Doug had to admit it looked a lot like his own footprint—in fact, exactly like it. It felt a little creepy. He made a note of the clue.

"Let's follow the trail back to the scene of the other two crimes and see what else we can find," Doug said. He and Skeeter retraced Doug's steps back to where he saw Connie earlier. There, in the dirt near the sidewalk, was another set of footprints, just like Doug's.

"Look at this," Doug said. "This set of prints is just like the last set."

"Yeah, they look just like yours," Skeeter honked.

"Skeeter, please!" Doug pleaded. "I know this person looks like me. But this has got to be some kind of evil twin or clone thing. And you can't have an evil twin who doesn't look like you. It doesn't work. Anyway, if this person is wearing shoes just like mine, he must have bought them at Shoes 'N Shoes. Let's get over there."

Doug and Skeeter walked over to the store and explained the situation to the manager, Mr. "Happy Feet" Green.

"What can I do for you boys?" Mr. Happy Feet asked. Looking down at their feet, he added, "Goodness me, Doug, I've sold a lot of shoes like yours today."

Doug looked meaningfully at Skeeter. "Who did you sell the shoes to?" Doug asked.

"Let's see," he said. "Roger Klotz and Willy White. You know, they both wear size 6."

"Hey! That's my size!" Doug exclaimed.

Doug made a note of everything Mr. Happy Feet had said. "One last question,

Mr. Happy Feet. Do you remember where they went after making their purchases?" he asked.

"Hmmm," the manager said. "Willy said he was going to the Mental Meltdown Video Arcade. Roger . . . I believe he went into the new electronics store next door. Yeah, that's it," he finished.

Doug and Skeeter decided to split up. Skeeter went to the Meltdown Arcade and found out that Willy blew all his cash on Astra Fleet Goon-Blaster and left.

When Doug checked out the electronics store, he learned that Roger had purchased the new CyberGuy 2000, a full-sized, radio-controlled robot with lifelike motion. "Very lifelike," the store manager assured Doug.

Doug and Skeeter began walking back home. Doug checked his notebook. "Let's see," he started. "Someone who looks just like me has been picking on all my friends. He wears the same type of shoe and shoe size that I do. And the only people who could have worn that type of shoe were Willy and Roger."

"And you," interjected Skeeter.

"I know," Doug said. "Evil twin, remember? Wait a minute—" Doug consulted his notebook once more. "Skeeter, I think I know who did it."

Will Doug ever meet his evil twin? Will they continue to wear matching outfits?

Doug ran back to the beetball field with Skeeter close behind.

"Doug, where are we going and why are we running?" Skeeter panted.

"We're going back to find Patti and Connie. I want to unmask my evil twin while everyone is there," Doug replied.

When they reached the beetball field, the team was getting ready to leave. "Patti! Connie!" Doug hollered. "Wait up! I think I've figured out what's really been going on."

"What are you talking about, Doug?" asked Patti, puzzled.

Doug started to explain but at that moment they all heard a cry for help. When they turned around, they saw Roger Klotz running as fast as he could. Not far

behind him was . . . Doug! No . . . Roger had a full-sized robot that looked almost exactly like Doug!

"I can't believe it!" gasped Connie.

"Me, either," said Skeeter.

"You really were telling the truth, weren't you, Doug!" said Patti. "I knew you couldn't do anything that mean."

"Don't just stand there gawking, help me out!" cried Roger. "This thing has gone berserk!"

By now the robot had treed Roger and was shaking the trunk hard.

"Quick, Roger, throw your jacket over its head," shouted Doug. "That will confuse it."

Roger threw the jacket down. While the robot tried to uncover itself, Skeeter crept up behind it and turned off the power switch. Roger stopped cowering and started to descend.

"I should have left you up there," Doug fumed.

"Don't be mad, Funnie," Roger said as he reached the ground. "It was just a joke. I wanted to see what it was

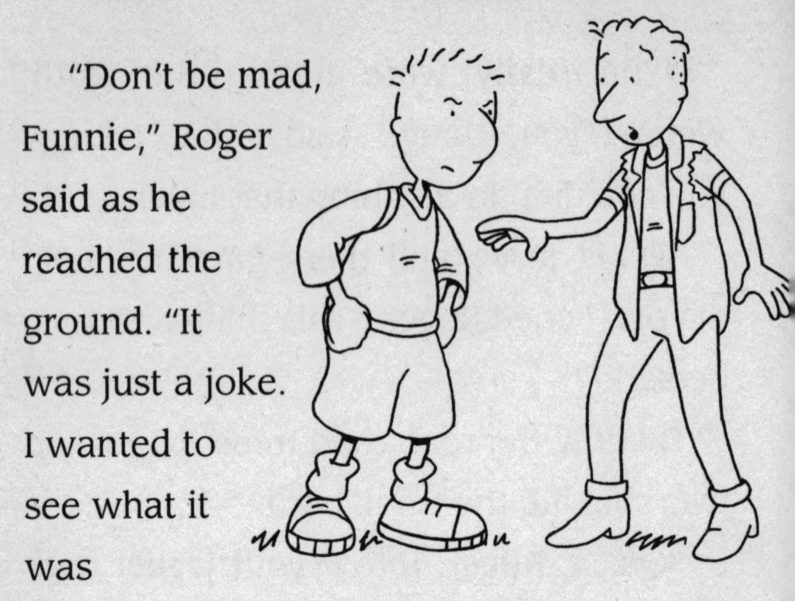

like to have you get in trouble instead of me, for a change. But the robot short-circuited or something and came after me. It didn't like playing pranks. I guess it's a goody-two-shoes, just like you!"

"I don't think that's much of an excuse for all the trouble you've put me through," Doug said.

"Oh, all right!" Roger gave in. "Say, why

don't I buy Frothy Goats for all of you to make up. My treat!"

"You should buy two for Doug," Patti said. "One for him and one for his evil twin."

They all walked off toward Swirly's, laughing.

5 Mysteries in 1

THE PLACE: Bluffington

THE MYSTERIES:

- The Case of the Baffling Beas
- The Last Boy on Earth
- The Mystery of the Robbed Rockers
- Dog Show Dilemma
- Puzzle of the Peanutty Buddy Money

Can Doug Funnie solve these mysteries and restore peace in Bluffington?

Find out in

FUNNIE MYSTERIES #3:
THE CASE OF THE BAFFLING BEAST

In Bookstores April 2000